Mary Blount Christian

SEBASTIAN
[Super Sleuth]
and the
Baffling Bigfoot

Illustrated by Lisa McCue

MACMILLAN PUBLISHING COMPANY
New York

COLLIER MACMILLAN PUBLISHERS
London

Remembering Sophie Perry

Macmillan Publishing Company
866 Third Avenue, New York, NY 10022
Collier Macmillan Canada, Inc.
First Edition
Printed in the United States of America

10   9   8   7   6   5   4   3   2   1

The text of this book is set in 12 point Primer.
The illustrations are rendered in scratchboard.

Library of Congress Cataloging-in-Publication Data
Christian, Mary Blount.
Sebastian (super sleuth) and the baffling bigfoot /
Mary Blount Christian; illustrated by Lisa McCue.—1st ed.
p.   cm.
Summary: Sebastian the dog and his detective master search
for Bigfoot and other suspects when a guest is attacked by
something "big and hairy" at the Sasquatch Inn.
ISBN 0-02-718215-0
[1. Mystery and detective stories.   2. Dogs—Fiction.
3. Hotels, motels, etc.—Fiction.]
I. McCue, Lisa, ill.   II. Title.
PZ7.C4528Scq   1990   [Fic]—dc20   89-13049   CIP   AC

Contents

1

The Unfortunate Cookie

Sebastian wiggled until he'd forced his thick body between the back of the station wagon seat and Lady Sharon. He touched his nose to her ear and grunted. It was time to trade windows. The drive had been long and boring, and he was tired of looking out the driver's side. Much to his embarrassment, Lady Sharon gave him a warm wet slurp on his fuzzy cheek before skittering to the window behind her human, Maude Culpepper, who was at the wheel.

The station wagon sped past a road sign advertising the House of Chicken. TEN TASTY TIDBITS OF CHUNKY CHICKEN, the sign said. Sebastian whimpered and wagged the stub of his tail. He didn't need any reminders that he was hungry!

Lady Sharon wiggled and wagged the stub of *her* tail. She leaned over to nuzzle Maude's neck.

"You two, sit," John commanded. "You shouldn't move about so much. It's distracting."

John—John Quincy Jones—was Sebastian's human and a detective with the City Police Department. Sebastian considered himself an undercover police dog, although he was unpaid. Not even a pat on the head or a "Job well done" did he get for solving cases too tough for humans to handle. It was John who got all the credit.

The two of them were on a well-deserved holiday from crime—and from Chief, their boss, who had nothing but unkind words for Sebastian (*flea bag* and *walking garbage disposal* being among them).

Now they whizzed past a sign for chili dogs. YOU'LL SIT UP AND BEG FOR MORE, it said. Even though the name made Sebastian a bit uncomfortable, he was willing to overlook it and stop there for some lunch. He groaned pitifully, hoping the humans would take the hint.

They didn't. "It was good of your sister to include me in the plans," Maude said to John.

"Jean's been wanting to meet you," John said. "Besides, she's looking for as big a crowd as she can get this weekend at Sasquatch Inn."

"Why'd she name it Sasquatch Inn?" Maude asked.

"That's the Indian name for Bigfoot," John said, laughing. "And there are always people claiming to have spotted Bigfoot around the area. If you ask me, their imaginations are working overtime."

Maude laughed, too. "Still, there's no harm in making the most of the rumors, I suppose. The notion that there's a seven-foot hairy monster roaming around the woods, leaving huge footprints, might scare off a few people, but I bet it would intrigue more and make them eager to try their own luck at spotting him."

John nodded. "Yeah. And I'm sure Jean will take advantage of every opportunity to make a go of the inn. It's still a week until the grand opening, but some writer from *Travelink* magazine is coming *this* weekend. Jean was a bit startled that he'd heard about the inn before she began to get the word out to the media. But who's going to ignore such good luck? Not Jean, anyway.

"The inn has been closed a couple of years, Jean said. I was wondering how she was going to fill it a week before the opening, but she said not to worry, that she would have a big surprise for all of us. Still, I wonder. Not everyone likes to stay in such a remote place. That's what caused it to fail before, I think."

"Hmmmm," Maude said. "Remote. Sounds ideal to me. I mean, assuming it's not too primitive."

The station wagon zoomed past a road sign advertising Barbie's Beef Barbecue. COWS JUST BEG TO BECOME OUR BARBECUE.

Sebastian turned onto his back and let his tongue hang out. He rolled his eyes pitifully and moaned. Surely John would take the hint.

He didn't. "Jean inherited the place from a distant relative of her husband on the condition that she make it a profitable business. She's got only two years to succeed, or she loses it to a lumber company. Jean didn't go into the details, but I had the distinct

3

feeling that she didn't want it to fall into other hands."

Maude gasped. "A *lumber* company! You mean someone would cut down this beautiful forest just for—for furniture and houses? That's awful."

John nodded, then laughed. "Well, if anyone can make the place successful, Jean can. She's got lots of energy and a talent for getting media attention. She was a high-powered publicity executive until she decided to get her kids out of the city."

"It'll be great for them, being raised far away from the pollution and problems of the city," Maude said. "Hey, are you getting hungry?" she asked. "All these road signs are reminding me that we haven't had any lunch yet."

At last! What would it be? Ten tasty tidbits of chunky chicken? Chili dogs that would make them sit up and beg for more? Barbie's Barbecued Beef that cows beg to become?

John pointed. "There's a sign. Yum Yum Chow Chinese Restaurant, a quarter of a mile down the road. Why don't we get take-out and eat in one of the roadside parks? That way the dogs can stretch their legs and run off some of that pent-up energy."

Sebastian curled his lip slightly. Chinese food wasn't his favorite. He didn't like those little stick-like things and knotty, hard disks—bamboo sprouts and sliced water chestnuts, he believed.

Maude pulled the station wagon onto the gravel

parking lot outside the restaurant, and John jumped out. "Shrimp fried rice okay with you?" he asked.

Sebastian sighed. Maybe he could pick out all the bits and pieces of shrimp and make a meal of it.

John returned with sacks of sweet-smelling food. They seemed awfully small to feed four! Maybe John and Maude weren't planning on eating much.

Maude drove several miles to a roadside park, where concrete tables and benches were scattered among some tall pine trees. She pulled out the pooch packs: knapsacks filled with a supply of water, bowls, and dry dog food. Dry! Would that woman never learn?

Lady Sharon nibbled daintily at the crunchy nuggets. Didn't she realize how tasteless that junk was? It was an affront to his finely tuned taste buds. Sebastian got under the picnic table, rested his chin on John's knee, and looked up at him soulfully. That look was usually good for a tidbit or two. And there were plenty more pathetic looks where it came from. Sometimes, when John wasn't looking, Sebastian practiced them in the mirror.

Maude clicked her chopsticks together and brought some of the shrimp mixture to her mouth. Sebastian waited anxiously to see if she would drop any.

"Tell me more about your sister," Maude said. "She's a widow, isn't she?"

John nodded, losing a few grains of rice from his

chopsticks. Sebastian gobbled them up. No need to leave evidence of John's sloppiness. It would only embarrass him, Sebastian figured.

"Yeah," John said. "Jean's husband died two years ago. She was all right financially, since she had a good job with a big firm. But I know it's been rough raising Barrie and JJ alone. Barrie, the girl, is ten. JJ is eight and a real handful."

"What's her last name again?" Maude asked.

"Wheeler," John replied. "She was so full of kooky publicity ideas that I used to call her Wheeler Dealer." He chuckled. "For instance, when she was publicizing one of those monster movies for a theater, she made a big deal of having a nurse and ambulance standing by. Then she hired a bunch of teenage girls to pretend to faint or run outside screaming. Everybody figured it was a hoax, but the movie made the front pages of both newspapers that day. And once she led an elephant right into city hall to publicize the circus." John laughed. "Took it upstairs in the elevator, too. She's a real character!"

"Well, I hope she doesn't have any such thing planned for us at Sasquatch Inn," Maude said, smiling. "I'm looking forward to a restful, peaceful weekend, myself."

"She wouldn't," John said. "She's older and wiser now." He laughed. "Older, anyway."

Sebastian grew tired of waiting for the tidbits that John dropped. He edged toward the crinkled cookie on the napkin next to John's elbow. *Snap!*

"Sebastian, no!" John yelled. "Not my fortune cookie!"

Sebastian grimaced as the cookie crumbled in his mouth and the taste of paper registered with him. *Yuk!* Why would anybody make cookies with paper in them? *Ptoooie!* He spat out the paper into John's hand.

Maude held her sides, laughing. "I can't believe Sebastian got your fortune!" She wiped a tear from the corner of her eye. "Well, if it's bad news, at least it's Sebastian's and not yours! What does it say?" she asked.

John held the paper by his thumb and forefinger. "Humph!" he said. "Sebastian can *have* this one. It says, 'Beware: Strangers mean dangers.'"

2
A Room with a View

During the sudden lull in conversation, Sebastian ate the rest of John's shrimp fried rice. Did they think that warning, "Strangers mean dangers," would frighten the old super sleuth? No way! He laughed in the face of danger. Danger was his life!

"What does *your* fortune cookie say, Maude?" John asked.

Maude smiled coyly. "It says, 'Kisses can change your name from Miss to Mrs.'"

John grabbed her hand. "I hope that means you will say yes soon."

Maude smiled at John in that ridiculous way.

Oh, yuk! Sebastian was hoping that John and Maude had forgotten all that silliness. As for the hairy hawkshaw, he was married to his work. There was no room in his life for domestic distractions.

They climbed back into the station wagon and made the rest of the trip without any further stops. As they neared the inn, they turned down a dirt road that snaked its way through tall trees and thick underbrush. It was so thick that, strain as he might,

9

Sebastian could barely see through it. A wooden signpost at the side said CAUTION. BIGFOOT XING.

John whooped. "Bigfoot Crossing. That Jean! That sign has her name written all over it."

"That's very funny," Maude said. "At least I *hope* it's a joke. I don't think I'm ready to see a big, hairy monster crossing the road."

"Oh, it's a joke, all right," John said. "Nobody really believes Bigfoot exists, surely!"

Maude slowed the station wagon as they passed under a sign that said WELCOME TO SASQUATCH INN, BIGFOOT TERRITORY. They were in a large parking lot crowded with cars, trucks, and vans. Two vans marked "Stuntmobile I" and "Stuntmobile II" were parked next to the huge, rustic building that was the inn.

"Well," John said, "it looks as if Jean was able to get a big crowd here, after all. But movie stuntmobiles? I guess that was the surprise she mentioned."

Maude pulled into a parking space and shut off the motor. "I don't think you should dismiss Bigfoot so quickly, John. There have been sightings all around the world. People have taken movies and still pictures of *something* big and hairy. I mean, what else could be seven feet tall?"

"A basketball player, maybe," John said. "It has to be something like that, don't you think?" he added, unfastening his seat belt. "Just practical jokes, hoaxes."

Maude crawled out of the car and stretched. "John, you don't really believe that, do you? I'm not a believer, but it's hard to discount so many stories about this monster. Some of the witnesses have been police, I recall." Maude shrugged her shoulders. "I hope you're right, John."

Sebastian leaped over the front seat and out of the car, with Lady Sharon close behind. John was right. If there really was a Bigfoot, why hadn't scientists said so? They didn't believe in it, either!

Romping into the nearby woods, Sebastian yipped playfully. A squirrel skittered up one of the trees and made guttural noises at him. Satisfied, Sebastian loped back to John. It felt good to stretch his legs.

John's sister, a prettier version of him, rushed from the building. A boy and girl ran close behind her. Jean threw her arms around John's neck and gave him a big kiss. "John! I'm so glad you came! And you brought Sebastian. The kids were afraid you might not bring him!"

Barrie and JJ tugged at John's arm, jumping up and down and shoving each other. "Uncle John! Uncle John!" JJ screamed.

John scooped them into his arms, laughing. "It's good to see all of you. Jean, you look great! JJ, Barrie, you've both grown another foot since I last saw you. Everyone, this is Maude. Maude, this is Jean and her gang."

Barrie scrambled from John's arms and gave

Sebastian a long scratch behind his right ear, then his left. Sebastian leaned into the scratches. *Ummmm.* Barrie did know how to make a dog happy. Sebastian's foot thumped with each stroke.

"Look, Barrie!" JJ squealed. "There's another one just like Sebastian!"

Humpt! Lady Sharon just like the old four-on-the-floor fuzzy detective? No way! She was certainly cunning—she was a *dog*, after all. But she lacked the skills that only he, Sebastian (Super Sleuth), possessed: deductive reasoning, the ability to read as well as any human, the— He could go on and on, of course, but modesty prevented him.

A young man in a fringed buckskin costume and coonskin cap came out to take the luggage. They followed him into the lobby, which had pictures of Bigfoot everywhere. It was abuzz with people.

"I'm glad you managed to get a good crowd this weekend," John said. "It ought to impress the magazine writer, all right. Which one is he? Maybe I can whisper a few words in his ear about the rustic charm."

Jean shrugged. "He's in his room, and he's been there most of the time since he arrived. He doesn't seem the least bit curious, as you'd expect a journalist to be." She sighed. "I'm afraid it's going to take more than whispering nice things to impress Jaspar Wolfe. He's been very unimpressed so far, and to think, I jumped at the chance when he asked to come this weekend. I even got this group here a week early."

She went behind the registration desk and pulled two keys from the wall. "I wanted the inn to look crowded and busy for his visit, so I called in a favor." She nodded toward a group of people, who were talking and laughing. "See that guy with the beard? That's Wilhelm Sweiback, the movie producer. I used to do publicity for his company.

"Over there, that redhead is Kaye Faye, the actress, and that's Biff Hunk, the star, and one of the stuntmen talking to her. I don't see Malcolm Barnes. He was here a little while ago. You remember him, don't you, John? He's been in dozens of monster movies—*The Green Glob from Venus, Ogres from Outer Space.*"

She handed a key to Maude. "Room 323, Maude. Ken will take your bags up." She turned back to John. "The moment I read in *Variety* that Wilhelm was making a Bigfoot movie, I contacted him about premiering it here. We agreed that it would be ideal for both of us, and I scheduled the opening of the lodge for next weekend, when he wanted the premiere to take place. But then, when Jaspar Wolfe said he was coming *this* weekend, I asked Wilhelm to move up the premiere. Wolfe acted really miffed, though, to find that I had other people here."

Jean turned the registration book around so Maude could sign in. "The movie's called *Son of*

Sasquatch. Perfect, huh? He rented rooms for his actors and staff and for critics from around the country. Even if they hate the movie, they're bound to mention Sasquatch Inn in their reviews. It'll be famous, and we won't even have to buy the publicity! With any luck the inn will be a success."

"I knew you'd figure out something," John said, laughing. "Just don't go pulling any of your weird stunts, okay?"

"Me?" Jean laughed, too. "Now, you know me better than that!"

"That's the trouble," John said. "I *do* know you."

"All that's behind me," Jean promised. "Besides, I have to do something to make Jaspar Wolfe like Sasquatch Inn. He arrived only a little while ago and has already complained about the weather, the traffic, the meal schedule, and even the color of his bedspread. I offered to show him around, but he said he was going to his miserable room and didn't want to be disturbed under any circumstances. It's going to be *some* weekend!"

Jean handed a key to John. "Room 204," she said. She leaned closer to John. "Your room is right next to Biff Hunk's room. Unfortunately, you're also next to Jaspar Wolfe."

"I can hardly wait," John said, sighing. "I'll take my own bags, Sis."

Sebastian trotted behind John to the elevator, where they waited until it finally groaned and creaked and slid to the first floor. The doors squeaked open and Ken, the bellman they'd met earlier, held the door for them, then stepped into the lobby. "Your friend's all settled in 323. Your room's to the right when you step off the elevator on two," he said cheerily. "I think you'll be *real* surprised at the view."

Sebastian's lips parted in a panting grin. A surprising view? He liked surprises—nice surprises, that is. But he couldn't help remembering the fortune cookie: "Strangers mean dangers." And this place was full of strangers.

At the room, John set down his suitcase and opened the door.

Sebastian scooted in and looked around. It was primitive, but not too primitive. The walls were rough-hewn wood, and the furniture was a bleached pine. A reproduction of a painting of Bigfoot hung over the bed. A braided rag rug in desert colors covered nearly the entire floor and matched the bedspread. If Jaspar Wolfe's room was anything like this one, he had no reason to complain.

John opened his suitcase and put away his toiletries. He hung up his shirts and pants, then opened the drawers of the dresser and put in his underwear and pajamas.

Sebastian sighed sympathetically. Poor humans. They had to carry around so much extra stuff when they traveled. Too bad for them that they didn't grow their coverings like dogs—and Bigfoot, he thought with a rumbling chuckle.

Sebastian rose on his hind legs and looked out the window. Ken had said they'd be surprised by the view. *Hmmmmm*, nice view. The trees were so tall that even from the second floor he couldn't see the tops of them. A shimmering of sunlight reflected on a lake that barely showed through the thick clusters of leaves. What looked like several narrow footpaths began at a clearing and disappeared into the thick underbrush almost immediately.

What was that? A slight movement in the underbrush caught Sebastian's attention. A huge brown dog? A bear, perhaps? Maybe it was a human wearing a fur coat. The weather was mild, but movie stars were fond of wearing animal furs in any sort of weather. The inn was certainly full of movie stars right now.

Sebastian shuddered. Whatever he had seen down there, it had looked pretty big from up here. Well, no matter. It was gone now.

Sebastian gazed lazily out the window, enjoying the peaceful scene. Suddenly the air was electrified by a high-pitched shriek. A woman ran from one of the paths, screaming and flailing her arms. She collapsed into the dirt.

3
So Much for Hogwash

Sebastian bounced and barked frantically. John rushed to his side and peered out the window. A crowd had already begun to gather around the woman below.

"Come on, fellow," John said as he whirled and raced toward the door.

He didn't have to ask Sebastian twice! As quick as a brown fox, Sebastian passed John in the hall. There was no time to wait for the elevator. The two of them raced toward a door marked with a red, lighted EXIT sign and bounded down the flight of stairs. They burst into the lobby and out the front door to where the crowd had gathered.

"No! No! Leave me alone!" the woman was screaming. Her eyes were squeezed shut, and she was flailing out at anyone who reached to help her up.

"Ma'am," John said quietly, "whatever frightened you isn't here now. It's all right, ma'am. Just try to sit up. My name is John Quincy Jones, Detective Jones. I'm a police officer, and I won't let anyone hurt you."

The woman stopped hitting out and screaming.

"Now let's just sit you up, ma'am," John said. "Get back, everybody," he said, motioning to the crowd.

Sebastian figured John meant the civilians, so he moved in closer.

The woman sniffled. She opened one eye slowly, then the other. She looked at John. Then she looked at Sebastian and screamed.

Sebastian backed up and sat on his haunches, puzzled. What was it about that friendly, fuzzy mug that could frighten her? Generally, it was only criminals who feared him.

Jean knelt beside the woman. "Mrs. Fauzio, are you all right? Should I call an ambulance? What happened?" She and John pulled Mrs. Fauzio to her feet. The woman leaned heavily on them as they led her back to the inn lobby and helped her into a chair. The crowd followed at a distance, muttering to one another.

"Jean, perhaps we should get Mrs. Fauzio some hot tea to calm her nerves," John suggested.

"Of course!" Jean said. "Ken! Oh, where is that fellow when I need him? Always slipping off from work! His days here are numbered. Never mind. I'll get it myself," she said.

While Jean rushed off to get Mrs. Fauzio a cup of hot tea, John sat with the woman. "Can you tell me what happened, ma'am?"

Mrs. Fauzio sighed wearily. "I—I'm not sure ex-

actly. I was out on one of the nature trails, bird-watching, when suddenly I was shoved face first into some underbrush and my purse was snatched."

"Yes?" John said. "Someone knocked you down and stole your purse?"

"Not some*one*," Mrs. Fauzio said. "Some*thing*. It was some*thing*.

"It was big, I think. And it was brown, sort of. Yes, that's it. It was big and brown. And it stole my purse. It just snatched it right off my arm and ran with it." Mrs. Fauzio suddenly gasped. "I was robbed by Bigfoot!"

The crowd murmured; whispers hissed like wind through pine needles. Wilhelm Sweiback's eyes glittered as he motioned to a young woman with a bouncy ponytail. "Peggy, call the wire services and the area television stations. Tell 'em that Bigfoot has gone on a rampage about the movie. Make it good. Say something about seeking revenge on us, stuff like that. That ought to be good for a thirty-second television item and maybe three or four inches in the papers."

"Please don't do this," John said. "You'll just muddle up the investigation. And you know as well as I do that there's no such thing as Bigfoot."

The young woman rushed off toward the phone without even answering John.

Sebastian figured that if he had to make a snap judgment about the culprit, he'd point to Wilhelm.

He was just trying to drum up publicity for his movie.

Jean had returned with the tea, and Mrs. Fauzio paused to sip it.

"Now, Mrs. Fauzio," John said, "there's no such thing as Bigfoot. You did say you were shoved face first, so you probably didn't get a good look at your assailant. Perhaps you're letting your imagination get the best of you."

John pulled Jean aside. "Jean, I hope you didn't have anything to do with this prank."

Jean blinked at her brother. "What kind of publicity do you think that would be, having one of my guests robbed? I'm afraid I'll lose guests, under the circumstances."

John patted her shoulder. "Of course, Jean. I'm sorry I accused you. But you should speak to your friend, Mr. Sweiback. He is certainly exploiting this."

"He's right," Jean told Mr. Sweiback. "I mean, it doesn't look good for the inn, and she *is* one of your people."

"One of *my* people?" Mr. Sweiback said. "I thought she was one of *your* invited guests."

All eyes turned to Mrs. Fauzio. "You're a gate-crasher?" Jean said.

Mrs. Fauzio opened her mouth as if to reply, but clamped it shut again, shrugging. She looked down at her hands, shaking her head sadly.

21

Jean rolled her eyes. All of this trouble from a gate-crasher.

John shrugged. "That's beside the point right now. You did assign her a room, so she seems to be a guest. No matter how she got here, the fact remains, it appears that she was pushed down and had her purse stolen. I think you'd better call the local representative of the law and report this."

"That would be Stan—er, Sheriff Stanford Tyler," Jean said, nodding. She blushed slightly.

John raised an eyebrow. "Do I detect something significant here?"

Sebastian had noticed it, too. It was the same sort of blush that John wore when he talked about Maude—and that Maude wore when she talked about John. Humans!

"Okay, maybe," Jean said. "He's been coming around a lot since we moved here."

No time for silliness. There was a mystery to be solved. As long as criminals didn't rest, neither could Sebastian (Super Sleuth)!

John had pooh-poohed Mrs. Fauzio's description of the perpetrator. But the cagey canine did recall seeing something big and brownish moving about in the woods just before Mrs. Fauzio ran out screaming. Maybe her description wasn't as far off as John thought.

Suddenly Sebastian's magnificent nose detected fudge brownies. He sniffed the air. Ah! Sebastian pushed through the door to the kitchen to find Barrie and JJ fighting over a single fudge brownie.

"Mine!" JJ yelled. "I'm the youngest! You're supposed to spoil me!"

"Mine, squirt," Barrie said. "I'm bigger and there's more room in me to fill up!"

Here now, Sebastian thought. That was no way for siblings to behave. He jumped up and snapped the fudge brownie off the plate, swallowing it whole. Now there was nothing to fight about!

"Ha, ha," JJ told Barrie, "now you don't get it."

"Nah, nah, nah," Barrie said, "you don't get it, either. So there!"

Jean burst through the door. "You two stop your arguing and get out of the kitchen. And take Sebastian with you. He shouldn't be in here."

"Come on, Sebastian," Barrie said. "Let's go look for the robber." She pushed the door open, and Sebastian galloped through. Now, there was a girl after his own heart! She understood—maybe.

"And stay out of the woods until Stan—er, ah, Sheriff Tyler gets here!" Jean called after them.

Surely she didn't mean him! Sebastian concluded. *He* had a job to do.

Sebastian trotted to the spot where Mrs. Fauzio had stumbled screaming from the woods. There were plenty of footprints in the rust-colored dust at the mouth of the trail. After all, nearly all the guests had come out when Mrs. Fauzio screamed. Not everyone, he remembered. He still hadn't seen that Malcolm fellow who played Bigfoot in the movie. Nor had he seen Jaspar Wolfe, the magazine writer. And Ken, the bellman, wasn't there when Jean wanted the tea for Mrs. Fauzio.

Sebastian skulked onto the trail, his nose to the ground, sniffing for clues. He cocked one ear as the bushes behind him rustled.

"Mom said not to go in there," JJ whispered. "You're going to get into such trouble! I'll tell."

"Am not!" Barrie growled in a stage whisper. "Mom said to watch Sebastian. That's what I'm doing. I can't help it if he goes in the woods."

"Then I'm coming, too!"

"Then come on! Just be quiet about it!"

Be quiet, indeed! Sebastian thought. Did they think this was a game? Sebastian put his belly to the ground and slunk along the trail cautiously.

"Shhh," Barrie said. "Let's play like Sebastian is on the trail of the robber, okay?"

"Shhh, yourself," JJ said.

Shhh, Sebastian thought.

They had gone perhaps ten yards into the thick woods when they heard a panting sound. *Huh, huh, huh.*

The hair on Sebastian's spine prickled. His whiskers bent forward. Someone big was breathing hard on the other side of the underbrush. Sebastian let out a throaty growl.

There was a muffled gasp, followed by a thump and the jangling of metal hitting metal. The bushes rippled briefly, then were still. The panting sound faded.

Sebastian let out his breath. *Wheeew.*

"Wheeew," JJ said.

"Wheeew," Barrie said.

Cautiously, Sebastian stuck his nose between the bristly branches of the shrubs. A leathery smell tickled his nose, and he growled.

Sebastian pushed his whole body through the underbrush. There on the ground lay a black leather purse. That must have been the noise he'd heard. Strewn about it were car keys, coins, several twenty-dollar bills, and a California driver's license with a picture of Mrs. Fauzio. There was something behind the license in the plastic jacket, but he couldn't work it out.

Wait a minute. The name on the license was Corinne Fayette. Why would she say her name was Fauzio but carry a license that said Fayette?

What Sebastian saw then made that question seem pretty unimportant. On the ground beside the purse, in the dust, was a footprint. And it was big. Really *big*!

4
Best Foot Forward

Sebastian stared at the footprint. He'd never seen anything so big. Who could have such a huge and unusually shaped foot? Look at the toes! Sebastian shuddered as a thought came to him. What if John was wrong? What if there really was a Bigfoot?

JJ stepped through the bush behind Sebastian. "Is that one of *ours*?" he asked Barrie.

"Don't be stupid!" Barrie said. "I didn't do it, unless you—"

"Don't be stupid!" JJ said.

They were both talking kind of stupid, Sebastian thought. They were just kids. They had little feet. How could they make such a big print?

"Don't call me stupid!" Barrie said, and she shoved JJ.

JJ shoved back, and soon the two were scuffling, kicking up dust. Before Sebastian could nudge them away, they had destroyed the footprint. Now there was no way to show John the evidence.

"Lemme alone," JJ said. "I'm gonna tell on you."

"Yeah," Barrie said, "and I'm gonna tell on you, too."

Sebastian had no stomach for their childish arguments; he had work to do. Pawing at the strewn contents of the purse, he worked them back inside. He would take the purse to John. John would be so glad to have it found. But who took the purse? Had that footprint been a clue? If so, how would he let John know about it, now that it had been destroyed?

"Hey!" JJ yelled. "Sebastian dug up some dirt with the purse. He covered up the footprint!"

Sebastian covered it up? Didn't those kids have any idea that it was they who— Oh, never mind. He snatched up the purse and galloped toward the inn with Barrie and JJ close behind.

Sebastian ran into the lobby, where John was talking to Mrs. Fauzio. A tall man wearing a khaki uni-

form and a star badge was there, too. Sebastian figured he was the sheriff who made Jean blush.

"My purse!" Mrs. Fauzio shrieked, pointing at Sebastian. "That's my purse!"

"I found it," JJ yelled. "I found Mrs. Fauzio's purse!"

"I found it first," Barrie said, poking her brother on the arm.

Ridiculous children! It was the old super sleuth who'd found it, in case they'd forgotten. Sebastian rose on his back legs, offering the purse to John.

John bent down and stroked Sebastian on the head. "It doesn't matter who found it. Just so it was found."

A man with coal black eyes, a pencil-thin mustache, and graying sideburns came into the lobby, frowning. "How can anyone rest with all this shouting going on?" he demanded. "My head is splitting. I can't see that this is helping your image any," he said, glaring at Jean.

"I'll get you some aspirin," Jean offered. "I'm sorry about the commotion, Mr. Wolfe."

Sebastian wondered how Jean could even be polite to such a nitpicking nagger.

"There's been an incident," John told Mr. Wolfe between clenched teeth. "Sheriff Tyler is trying to help this lady, so if you will be so kind as to *sit* down—"

Jaspar Wolfe looked startled, but he plopped into

a chair immediately. All attention returned to Mrs. Fauzio.

"Check the contents," Sheriff Tyler instructed Mrs. Fauzio. "See if there's anything missing."

Mrs. Fauzio glanced into the purse. "Everything's here."

"Are you sure?" Sheriff Tyler asked. "Perhaps you should dump the contents on the table and study them a moment."

"That won't be necessary," she insisted.

Sebastian was sure she didn't want them to see her driver's license with the name Fayette on it. Also, she hadn't said she'd had binoculars stolen, and she didn't have any now, although she'd said she was a birdwatcher. But why would she lie? And why was she going by a phony name? Had she faked the theft? Why? And if she had, who, or what, had they heard in the woods?

"There was a footprint by the purse, too," JJ said. "But Sebastian messed it up, digging."

Errrrr, Sebastian complained.

"But I can describe it," JJ said. "It was about six feet long—"

Loud murmurings erupted among the critics and movie people.

"Was not!" Barrie said. "It was only about fourteen inches long."

"And three feet wide," JJ continued, pausing only to stick out his tongue and cross his eyes at his sister.

The murmurings became anxious babblings.

"Was not!" Barrie said again. "It was only about nine inches across."

John shook his head. "You kids quit making up these silly tales. You're getting about as bad as your mother with these wild Bigfoot stories."

Sheriff Tyler cleared his throat and stuck the pencil he was using behind his ear. "Actually, there *have* been rumors about Bigfoot sightings around here off and on for many years."

The babbling became shouts. "Bigfoot's real!" someone shouted.

John looked exasperated. "But surely you don't believe—"

"I'm only saying that the sheriff's files are full of reports and investigations into the claims. But none of them came to anything."

"Of course not," John said.

Several of the people—the critics, mostly—rushed to the telephones. Sebastian figured they were calling their own newspapers and television stations, making sure they had news scoops. Soon they returned.

Jean came out of the kitchen. "Johnson, our chef, informs me that supper is about to be served, folks. Stan, won't you join us for supper and continue your investigation afterward? It'd be a shame to pass up good barbecued ribs." Jean's eyes seemed to sparkle when she looked at Sheriff Tyler. And Sebastian noticed that the sheriff broke into a broad grin whenever he looked at *her*.

Sheriff Tyler accepted the invitation, which was no surprise to the alert canine. "It might be easier to talk to folks once they've had something to eat, anyway."

Sebastian couldn't agree more! He figured he'd be able to investigate better after he'd had something to eat, too.

The sheriff turned to John. "I'd appreciate your big-city expertise on this, John. I've been sheriff for only a couple of months, and the worst thing I've had to find out so far has been who knocked down all the mailboxes on Farm Road 896."

He chuckled. "That one was easy to solve. The kid left his truck's license plate embedded in the last mailbox. All I had to do was look up the owner."

Sebastian edged a little closer. What about *his* help? Maybe this guy just didn't realize it was he, Sebastian (Super Sleuth), who actually solved all of John's cases.

Jean turned to Barrie. "Take Sebastian to the back porch and feed him," she said. "And ring the dinner bell so the rest of the guests will come to dinner."

Sebastian was indignant that he wasn't to eat in the dining room and that he wasn't getting barbecued ribs. That was no way to treat him! Still, he wasn't too proud to eat wherever—and whatever— he was fed. He had to keep up his strength if he was to discover who had snatched Mrs. Fauzio's purse and why she was using a false name on her license. And why she was at the inn, in the first place. She was definitely not a birdwatcher, and she was not an invited guest. Also, of course, there was that big footprint. And the missing Ken.

Barrie led Sebastian through the dining room and kitchen and out to the back porch, where two bowls of food waited. That was fine for him. But what was Lady Sharon to eat?

John followed them. "Behave yourself, Sebastian."

Maude came out with Lady Sharon. "Wow, what a good nap I had," she said, stretching lazily. "I didn't wake up until the dinner bell. What a wonderfully peaceful place this is."

John broke into laughter, and Sebastian's lips split into a panting grin. Peaceful? Did she have a lot to catch up on!

5
Little Sneakers and Big Foot

Sebastian nudged his bowl a distance from Lady Sharon's. He didn't want her getting the idea that she could have any of *his* supper. A detective needs to feed his brain cells, especially when he has so much to investigate.

While he munched, he thought through what he'd heard and seen. As he had looked at the scenery, he'd seen Mrs. Fauzio stumble from the woods in a real fright. She'd been robbed of her purse, and she'd insisted that something big and hairy, like Bigfoot, had taken it. If there was no such thing as Bigfoot, what had made the big footprint in the woods? Suddenly Sebastian thought about something else. Why had he been looking out the window in the first place?

Ken! Ken, the bellman, had said they'd be real surprised by the scenery. Had that been the surprise he was talking about? Had he known that Mrs. Fauzio would be robbed? And how would he have known, unless he was in on it? He had had time to get from the lobby into the woods. Or had he been talking only about the pretty trees and the lake? Ken had been missing when they'd brought Mrs. Fauzio into the lobby. He hadn't answered Jean's call. Of course, that magazine writer, Jaspar Wolfe, had not been around, either. Supposedly he'd been in his room; he'd asked not to be disturbed. But was that because he hadn't really been there and didn't want anyone to know?

And Jean had mentioned that someone else was missing, too. Oh, yes, the movie actor who'd played Bigfoot in *Son of Sasquatch*. Was he *still* playing Bigfoot? Or had Mrs. Fauzio, alias Mrs. Fayette, made up the whole thing? What might be her motive?

If Sebastian had learned anything during his career, it was that where there was crime, there were means, opportunity, and motive. No money was missing from the purse, so robbery was not the motive. Was it publicity, as John suspected? Then the finger of accusation would still point to the movie producer—or even to Jean.

Somehow Sebastian thought it must be more than publicity. A thief might have taken Mrs. Fauzio's keys, intending to steal her car later. Certainly he or she would have taken the money. Perhaps the thief had been running and dropped the purse on hearing Sebastian and the children in the woods. But why would the thief have been in the woods after all that time? And how could he or she have left such a large footprint? What if there really was a Bigfoot? What if it had taken Mrs. Fauzio's purse out of curiosity, then thrown it away when it no longer held his interest?

Sebastian dismissed the whole idea of Bigfoot. He was letting the silly talk get to him. There was a logical explanation to all of this. He just had to find it.

He cleaned the last drop of food from his bowl. Now, if he could just sneak away from Lady Sharon.

Woooof! She nudged him, then playfully ran around him in circles, making mock growls and barks. Slapping the ground with her front paws, she wagged her stub of a tail. Lady Sharon was ready for a game of chase.

There was nothing to do but join her. Besides, he needed to exercise a bit, keep those fine muscles toned, just in case he needed to make a fast getaway or to chase down a fleeing criminal.

Sebastian wagged the stub of his tail and took off running, with Lady Sharon close behind. He led her to the big rustic barn in back of the inn and circled it several times. She was still too close for him to slip away. Quickly he stopped and spun around. Lady Sharon skidded to a halt and, with a gleeful expression, took off running in the other direction. Sebastian pretended to chase her, but gradually he slowed down until she had rounded a corner of the barn and was out of sight.

Quickly he ducked inside the barn door. Let her

chase shadows for a while, he thought. What Sebastian had to do was wander around the dining room and see what he could find out. For this he had to have a disguise. Jean had made it clear that dogs belonged outside, away from the barbecue. But what could he use?

Sebastian strolled through the barn, letting his keen mind absorb its contents. At one end were the horse stalls and a wagon. On the wall was a buckskin suit similar to the one Ken had been wearing when he was last seen. Maybe it *was* Ken's. That might be a good disguise, if he found nothing better. Also, there were an old lantern and great piles of hay, probably for feeding the horses and for lining the wagon for hayrides. He couldn't begin to understand it, but humans seemed fond of riding around on top of hay in a bumpy wagon.

What was that sticking out from the hay? It looked like a piece of wood, or maybe stiff leather. What was it doing in the hay? Sebastian tugged at it. At last it moved, leaving Sebastian and the strange object sprawled on the barn floor.

Sebastian stared at the thing. It was something like a boot. Only the sole of it looked just like the bottom of a big foot. Big foot? *Bigfoot!* Sebastian put one paw into the boot and walked in the soft barn dirt. He looked back. Sure enough, that was the footprint they'd thought was Bigfoot's. It had been made by this very boot.

Sebastian felt much better. Now he could laugh at himself for getting fooled, however briefly, by the stories about Bigfoot.

But who had made the footprint? Each of the kids had denied doing it.

About that time, Lady Sharon bounded into the barn, yipping and excited. She'd finally figured out that Sebastian had left her to chase her own shadow. She'd brought Barrie and JJ with her.

"Oh, no!" JJ yelled. "Barrie, Sebastian has found our footprinter. If Mama finds out, she'll—"

"Finds out what?" Jean asked. She and John and Maude were standing behind them, staring. The sheriff stood close by, too. "It's a good thing I missed you two after the main course and got curious," Jean added.

"Uh-oh," JJ said. "Too late now!"

"Finds out *what*?" Jean asked again.

John stepped forward, with Maude close behind. "What's that thing Sebastian has caught his foot in?" He bent to lift Sebastian's foot out of the boot.

Maude peeked over John's shoulder. "What *is* it?"

Sputtering, John stood up, holding the boot. "Jean, you promised me that you weren't pulling anything funny here. You promised!"

Jean looked bewildered. "But I—I've never seen this thing before."

Barrie started bawling. "She didn't know about this, honest, Uncle John."

JJ joined in, too. "Honest, Uncle John."

Sebastian knew that crying routine was to get sympathy and avoid punishment. If *he* were in trouble—and thank goodness he wasn't—he would have looked hangdog.

"Never mind that now," John said. "Just tell me quickly, before I lose my temper."

Barrie sniffled. "JJ and I found that boot in the barn when we were exploring. We thought it would be fun to play a trick on everybody. We didn't mean any harm."

"But why did you play that mean trick on Mrs. Fauzio?" Jean demanded to know.

"Oh, no!" Barrie said. "We didn't do that, Mama! And we didn't make the footprint that Sebastian ruined, either. Honest!"

Sebastian rumbled under his breath. Why did they insist that *he* had destroyed the evidence, when it was those two who'd done it, scuffling and carrying on?

"We found it out here one day. We thought it would be funny to put some footprints down by the lake in the soft mud," JJ said. "But we never got a chance."

"It was probably left by some prankster, perhaps the last owners of the Sasquatch Inn. All the same," Sheriff Tyler said, "I think it would be better if this boot were locked up somewhere so we won't have any such pranks."

"You're right, Stan," Jean said. "I'll put it in the empty storage room. I'll even give you the key, if that will make you feel better about it."

Stan smiled at Jean. "You keep the key, Jean. Of course I trust you."

As they started back to the inn, Jean said, "You know, I've been thinking. With some remodeling, the barn would make a wonderful Bigfoot museum. This boot could be one of the displays about hoaxes. People staying at the inn could come in free. Other people might pay a dollar or so and—"

John laughed. "I might know you'd take a lemon and make lemonade, Jean. Or should I say, turn myth into a moneymaker."

"I hope you're right," Jean said. "I really want to make this inn thrive. And I've got only two years to do it, too."

"And if Jean loses the inn, we all lose," Sheriff Tyler said. "Because that greedy tree pirate, J. A. Spar, will be entitled to the land. He'll turn all this beautiful wooded area into yet another satellite of Sparton Industrial Forest. He'll strip it of every single tree."

"It'll destroy the whole ecological chain out here," Jean said. "Where will the birds and animals live? What will they eat? Spar has to be a jerk."

Didn't that man know that the earth needs friends, not enemies? Sebastian trotted behind Jean, staring at the boot she carried. If he could just solve

41

the mystery, Jean would have a chance to make the inn a nice place to stay. Then Mr. Spar wouldn't be able to get his hands on it and ruin the land.

Sebastian squinted at the boot. Something about it just didn't seem right. Then it hit him. The boot was for the *right* foot. The print in the forest had been a *left* foot. Was there a mate to this boot? If so, who had it? Or had the print in the woods been made by the real Bigfoot?

6
The Fortune Comes True

Sebastian followed the others only as far as the back porch of the inn before dropping into the shadows. It was undercover time, time for a disguise. Quickly he retraced his steps to the barn and wiggled into the pioneer outfit that he'd seen there. The old fuzzy detective needed some answers, and eavesdropping seemed the best way to get them.

Slipping into the kitchen, he started for the door to the dining hall, when suddenly someone tapped him on the shoulder. "Move your bag o' bones into high gear and get those dishes cleaned up, Ken," Johnson, the chef, said.

Sebastian skidded to a full stop. Bones? Had he said bones? Where?

"We got to serve coffee and petit fours in the lobby in a few minutes, and you haven't even cleared the dining room yet. Where've you been hiding since you set up the dining room, lazy?"

Huh, huh, Sebastian grunted. If coffee and petit fours were being served in the lobby, then people would be hanging around there. And that would mean plenty of talk to listen to. Meanwhile, he didn't mind at all cleaning up the dishes. He remembered that barbecued ribs were the main course, and now he smelled leftover ranch-style baked beans, and baked potatoes with sour cream, chives, melted cheese, and bacon bits. Yummy!

While the bossy guy busied himself arranging the tiny iced cakes on a tray, Sebastian lugged dish after dish into the kitchen and licked them sparkling clean. Who needed soap and water when there was a fantastic tongue like his?

"Good job!" the bossy guy said when he looked around. "Now take this tray of petit fours into the lobby, and I'll take the coffee. I already put the cups out there while everyone was eating."

Sebastian's nose quivered as the delicious sweet smells drifted from the tray. He inhaled deeply before setting the tray on a table near a wall. Almost immediately, the guests stopped milling about and came to hover near the table.

Well, what the heck? They wouldn't miss one little cake square. He snapped up the nearest square, then stepped back before those gluttonous humans got to them.

Sebastian wandered among the guests, listening to bits and snatches of conversation. "We should be on the eleven o'clock news, Mr. Sweiback," the ponytailed girl said. "By morning, there'll be plenty of cameras here, too."

"Biff, are you all set to save me from Bigfoot

again?" Kaye Faye teased. "I'm counting on you."

"You can count me out if the real one shows up," he said. "I don't think my insurance pays for incidents off the movie set."

"I am bored, bored, bored!" Jaspar Wolfe complained. "My room is supposed to overlook the lake, and I can't even see the lake for all those stupid trees. Wouldn't you think they'd cut some trees for a better view? And the decor is tacky, tacky, tacky."

Lady Sharon left Maude's side and came over to sniff Sebastian's coonskin cap, but a throaty growl sent her scurrying back to Maude.

When all the people had served themselves coffee and petit fours, Jean said, "Attention, everyone. Many of you have been asking a lot of questions about the inn and about Bigfoot, so one of the traditions the inn will have—starting tonight—is an informal discussion over our coffee and dessert in the evenings."

The crowd of people located chairs and settled in them—all except Kaye Faye, who strolled casually toward the door.

Sebastian eased himself into a shadowy corner and waited.

"This inn, according to legend, was built on a Bigfoot campsite. And the legend says the monster still roams near here, waiting to reclaim his home." Jean threw a sideward glance at John. "Of course, it's only a *story*."

There was muttering among the guests. Then one raised her hand. "What *does* Bigfoot look like?"

"Descriptions of Bigfoot vary," Jean said. "It could be from six to ten feet tall. It might weigh up to five hundred pounds. It's usually described as reddish brown, with hair everywhere except for the soles of its feet, its palms, and its face."

"But what about the footprint?" Maude asked.

"It could be from ten to seventeen inches long and maybe seven inches wide. The big toe and second toe are said to be separated from the others. Bigfoot makes a sound like a baby crying, and it walks on its two feet, swinging its arms like a man."

Sebastian huddled in his shadow, thinking. Whatever had been on the other side of the brush had sort of groaned and panted. It certainly hadn't sounded like a baby!

Mrs. Fauzio spoke up. "Does it eat people?"

Jean smiled. "No, Mrs. Fauzio. It eats berries, vegetables, fruit, leaves, and if it was ever desperately hungry, it might eat a small animal."

Animal? How small? A mouse? An English sheepdog? If Sebastian had been convinced that there was no Bigfoot, he no longer was.

"It has been called curious," Jean said. "And even mischievous, although I think what we consider pranks are really evidence of its curiosity."

"Like what?" John asked. Was he getting caught up in the fantasy, too?

"Well, there are stories that Bigfoot has stolen tents, backpacks, and even rubber rafts from campers. Later the people would find these items jammed into trees or behind rocks many miles from where they were taken."

Sebastian broke into a panting smile, and the crowd of people chuckled in unison.

"I think once his curiosity about these things was satisfied, Bigfoot discarded them. I don't think he's smart enough to pull pranks. But that might explain your purse, Mrs. Fauzio," Jean said. "He was just curious."

John cleared his throat loudly, frowning at Jean.

She shrugged. "That is, if there really is a Bigfoot. Some say it's just a hoax perpetrated by people who are silly, bored, or greedy."

John nodded, as if satisfied.

"Oh," Jean said. "There's one other thing I forgot to mention about Bigfoot. People say that there's a sharp, strong odor when he's around. And now we have a treat for you," she added. "A very *special* surprise."

Sebastian rumbled under his breath. He hadn't liked any of the surprises so far. He wasn't sure he wanted another.

Suddenly several of the guests shrieked and pointed toward the window near Sebastian.

Sebastian looked. Just on the other side of the window he saw a huge hairy creature—Bigfoot!

7
The Solution – or Is It?

Sebastian could feel the hair on his back stand up as a shudder made its way from his tail up to his neck. With a low rumble in his throat, he backed away slowly from the window. People were shrieking and bumping into one another in the effort to get as far away from the window as possible. Lady Sharon stood behind Maude, who stood behind John.

The door burst open, and the creature rushed into the lobby and picked up Kaye Faye, who screamed and beat her fists against it. Sebastian didn't like what he had to do, but he sprang forward, sinking his teeth into the leg of the beast.

"Ow!" Bigfoot shouted, to Sebastian's surprise, and dropped Kaye Faye.

"Hey!" Biff Hunk yelled. "I was supposed to save her, not *that* guy!"

"Idiot!" Kaye Faye said, and kicked Bigfoot in the shin.

"Ow!" Bigfoot shouted again. He rubbed his shin.

Sebastian settled back on his haunches and stared.

Wilhelm Sweiback called out, "That costume's worth a fortune! What if we make a sequel? Don't let that guy ruin it!"

"Please, people," Jean said, motioning for them to calm down, "I'm sorry you were frightened. This is not what you think! Please, be seated."

Bigfoot lumbered over to stand by Jean, and in one swoop removed its head! A huge sigh sounded loudly as the guests quieted enough to see that this was a real person in a Bigfoot outfit.

"Meet Malcolm Barnes," Jean said. "He plays Bigfoot in *Son of Sasquatch*. He and the other stars," she said, pointing toward Kaye Faye, who was being helped to her feet by Biff Hunk, "are here to answer your questions about the movie. The press conference is now open."

One of the critics stood. "Was it tough playing Bigfoot?" he asked.

"It got plenty *hot* in this outfit," Malcolm said. "Actually we had three Bigfoot outfits, since the movie called for Bigfoot's going into the water a couple of times. Unfortunately, one of them was stolen."

"Why wasn't I told?" Sheriff Tyler asked. "That might have some bearing on this case."

Wilhelm Sweiback waved off his question. "We reported it to our insurance company. We got a ransom note on it. It was stolen on location in the

Sparton Industrial Forest in central California about a month ago. That's why we didn't report it to you, sheriff."

Sparton Industrial Forest? Where had Sebastian heard that name before? Wasn't that the company that would take over if Jean failed? Was it merely coincidence, or was it significant?

"What about conflict on the sets?" a man asked Malcolm Barnes. "I hear that you wanted your name listed over Biff Hunk's and threatened to walk off the set, and that the stuntman was there as a warning that you could be replaced and nobody would ever know the difference."

Hmm, Sebastian thought. A motive?

"But what about that Bigfoot robbery this morning?" a woman asked. "Wasn't that just a publicity stunt?"

"We don't mind using whatever's available to us," Wilhelm said. "And it couldn't have been more timely. But, no, we didn't stage that episode. And now the conference is over, ladies and gentlemen. Thank you for your questions. We'll see you tomorrow."

Jaspar Wolfe leaned toward one of the critics. "They should probably give this place back to Bigfoot. If he would take Mrs. Fayette's purse, he might even do some real damage."

Sebastian's ears pricked up. Had he said Mrs. Fayette? Until now the old sleuth had thought only he and Mrs. Fayette knew she wasn't Mrs. Fauzio. Was this man in on it, too? Or did he know her name because it was he who had stolen the purse?

According to Jean, no incidents had occurred until the guests had arrived. Yet the Bigfoot outfit had been stolen in Hollywood. The people with the movie were the only ones who had been in both places. Of course, Mrs. Fayette had a California driver's license, so *she* might have been in both places. That would let the critics and Mr. Wolfe off the suspect list. Yet Jaspar Wolfe knew Mrs. Fayette's real name.

Mr. Sweiback had invited the critics. Jean had invited Mr. Sweiback and his entourage. The only uninvited guests, then, were Mrs. Fayette and Jaspar Wolfe. How she got here and why were still a mystery. But *he* had called Jean. Also, he'd insisted on coming a week before the place opened and had been miffed to find the others there.

What was the name of that magazine he represented? *Travelink.* It was a reputable magazine, Sebastian was sure. He had seen it many times on the newsstands. But was Wolfe a reputable writer?

John called Sebastian. "I wonder where he's gone to now," he said, not realizing that the old sleuth was right beside him, dandily disguised as a frontier bellman.

Discovering it was bedtime, Sebastian hastily retreated to a dark corner of the dining room, where he shook off the disguise. Then he joined John.

"Ah, there you are, boy. I suppose you've been out rooting up rabbits or some silly sport, huh? Well, let's trot off to bed now. Tomorrow will be a busy day, if I'm to solve this puzzling mystery."

Obediently, Sebastian followed John to their room, chuckling under his breath. It would be a grand day, indeed, when *John* solved a mystery! No, it was up to the hairy hawkshaw to do that.

When John was sound asleep, Sebastian tried to open the door to leave. His scratchings awakened John, but not completely. Still half-asleep, John groggily got up and opened the door for Sebastian— just the way he did at home!

Sebastian skittered through the hall and down the stairs. When he was sure that there was no one around, he sneaked behind the registration desk. He put his front paws up on the desk and studied the guest register. There was a phone number for *Travelink* magazine beside Jaspar Wolfe's name. Sebastian found a pencil. He knocked the phone from its cradle. Then, clutching the pencil between his teeth, he punched the telephone number. The magazine probably had a twenty-four-hour switchboard, or at least an answering service.

Sometimes he wished his paws were more like human hands, it was so difficult to do certain things. Still, he wouldn't want to trade his canine cleverness for hands.

"*Travelink* magazine," a woman answered. "Editorial department."

Suddenly it occurred to Sebastian that although he understood human language completely—even with all its strange grammatical quirkiness—he could not speak it!

"Hello?" the woman said. "Hello?"

Desperately Sebastian rolled his tongue across his teeth, took a deep breath, and said, *Wooof!*

"Wolfe, you say? There's nobody working here by that name. Sorry."

Nobody there by that name? If Wolfe wasn't a magazine writer, then who was he? Had *he*, too, lied about his name? What could be his motive? If the inn was ruined, then J. A. Spar would be the *only* person who would benefit. J. A. Spar. JASpar. Jaspar! Jaspar Wolfe!

This was no travel writer. This was the man who was trying to get the inn from Jean! Sebastian just had to wait for his chance to expose the rotter.

It came early the next morning. Sebastian was standing beside John and Maude when Jaspar Wolfe, or J. A. Spar, came down to buy a newspaper. As soon as he'd opened his wallet, Sebastian made a great leap, dislodging it from his hand.

He stared at the open wallet. He was right!

"Sebastian!" John scolded. "I'm so sorry! I don't know what got into my dog. Let me get that for—"

John stared at the driver's license. "J. A. Spar? You're—but—"

Mr. Spar sputtered so hard that his pencil-slim mustache slid to one side and hung there like a caterpillar on a trapeze.

"Jean," John said. "I think you'd better call Sheriff Tyler at once. I believe he has a suspect to question."

"I already have, John. I—"

"But I didn't take Mrs. Fayette's purse!" Mr. Spar said.

"Who is Mrs. Fayette?" John asked.

"I am!" Mrs. Fauzio said. "And only the person who stole my purse would know that."

Plus one clever canine.

"But—" John said.

"I'm an investigator with Apex Insurance Company," Mrs. Fayette said. She opened her wallet and pulled a card from behind her license. It identified her. "My company doesn't take kindly to missing Bigfoot costumes when they're insured by us for a half million dollars each. I thought it was someone in the movie company and hoped to track down the culprit here. I had no idea it was going to turn out to be this *tree butcher*."

Jean nodded. "Mrs. Fayette confided in me first thing this morning, so during breakfast I let her into Room 202. We found an interesting hairy suit hanging in the closet. I called Stan right away."

When Sheriff Tyler arrived seconds later, Mr. Spar confessed that he had taken the suit while the movie people were on location in the forest his company owned. He had planned to terrorize Jean into shutting down the inn before it even opened, thereby inheriting the land. But he had not counted on her bringing other guests there, especially the very ones he'd stolen the costume from. And certainly he hadn't expected to come up against an insurance investigator or a cagey canine detective.

"I was in the woods when I heard a horrible growl," Spar said. "I dropped the purse and ran. I figured it was safer to come back to the inn, in case there really was a Bigfoot out there."

Sebastian remembered growling. It must have been the old hairy hawkshaw who had scared Spar out there. By accident he had stopped the crime from escalating into something major! And what a relief to know that there was no real Bigfoot.

With that in mind, Sebastian thoroughly enjoyed the movie premiere that night. And the next day he found that Jean had been right. The inn was mentioned in every single newspaper story.

By the time they had packed to leave, Ken was back, complaining about fleas in his costume. Jean said he would be faster now, at least. And calls for reservations were coming in. The inn would surely be a success.

Sebastian wagged the stub of his tail and barked

a fond good-bye to Jean and the kids. Lady Sharon yipped happily and leaped into the station wagon. Then Maude turned it around and headed down the bumpy dirt road toward the highway and past the Bigfoot crossing sign.

John laughed. "Bigfoot crossing! That Jean! Some jokester!"

Sebastian hung his head out the window, sniffing the pine scent. Suddenly his keen nose caught the most awful smell.

"Phew!" John said. "There must be a skunk close by."

Sebastian caught sight of something moving among the thick underbrush. It was big and brown. He couldn't quite make it out, but he felt sure he'd heard the cry of a baby.

Sebastian's lips parted in a panting grin. A hoax? A practical joke? Maybe. But then again, maybe not. Just because there were people who didn't believe in Bigfoot didn't mean he wasn't real. After all, there were still some who didn't believe in Sebastian (Super Sleuth), either.

And, boy, were they wrong!